Pebble® Plus

Construction Zone

Construction Crews

by JoAnn Early Macken

Consulting Editor: Gail Saunders-Smith, PhD

Consultant: Don Matson, owner
Metro Construction, Paving, and Excavating
Roseville, Minnesota

Capstone
press®

Mankato, Minnesota

Pebble Plus is published by Capstone Press,
151 Good Counsel Drive, P.O. Box 669, Mankato, Minnesota 56002.
www.capstonepress.com

1 2 3 4 5 6 13 12 11 10 09 08

Library of Congress Cataloging-in-Publication Data
Macken, JoAnn Early, 1953–
    Construction crews/by JoAnn Early Macken.
    p. cm. — (Pebble plus. Construction zone)
    Summary: "Simple text and photographs present a construction crew, including information on the tools
and equipment they use" — Provided by publisher.
    Includes bibliographical references and index.
    ISBN-13: 978-1-4296-1235-7 (hardcover)
    ISBN-10: 1-4296-1235-5 (hardcover)
    1. Building — Juvenile literature. 2. Construction workers — Juvenile literature. I. Title. II. Series.
TH149.M33 2008
690 — dc22   2007027109

Editorial Credits
Sarah L. Schuette, editor; Patrick Dentinger, designer; Jo Miller, photo researcher

Photo Credits
Alamy/Roger Hutchings, cover; Stock Connection Blue, 7
Dreamstime/Christine Gonsalves, 1; Lisa F. Young, 15; Pryzmat, 5
Getty Images Inc./Stone/Peter Cade, 19; Uppercut Images/Pete Salutos, 21
iStockphoto/Lisa F. Young, 9; Robert Cocquyt, 13
Shutterstock/Ashley Whitworth, cover (sky); Brian McEntire, 17; Dwight Smith, 11

Note to Parents and Teachers

The Construction Zone set supports national science standards related to understanding
science and technology. This book describes and illustrates construction crews. The
images support early readers in understanding the text. The repetition of words and
phrases helps early readers learn new words. This book also introduces early readers
to subject-specific vocabulary words, which are defined in the Glossary section. Early
readers may need assistance to read some words and to use the Table of Contents,
Glossary, Read More, Internet Sites, and Index sections of the book.

Table of Contents

Working Together

Construction crews work together at job sites. They build roads, buildings, bridges, and homes.

Supervisors make sure
jobs go smoothly.
They meet with the crew
to go over plans.

Outside Jobs

Drivers operate trucks
and other heavy equipment.
They lift steel bars
with cranes.

Ironworkers build frames
to hold up the buildings.
They weld and bolt
steel bars together.

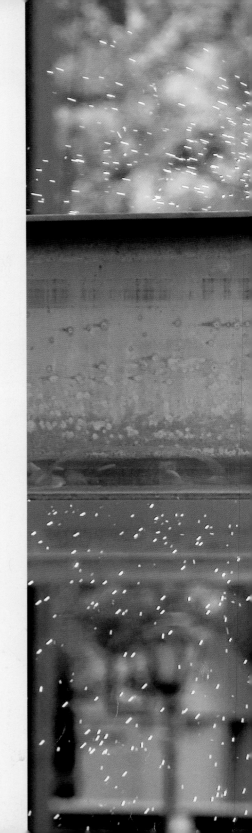

Bricklayers build walls

with bricks

or concrete blocks.

Finishing Work

Plumbers put water pipes
in the building.
Electricians install the lights
and turn on the power.

Inside, painters paint
the walls.
Carpenters put in floors,
stairs, windows, and doors.

Outside, roofers
put on shingles.
The rest of the crew
finishes their jobs.

19

More Jobs

Construction crews
start new jobs
all the time.

Glossary

concrete — a mixture of cement, water, sand, and gravel that hardens when it dries

crane — a machine with a long arm used to lift and move heavy objects

frame — the base that a building is built around; steel frames give support and shape to tall buildings.

install — to put something in place, ready to be used

shingles — a thin, flat piece of wood or other material used to cover roofs or outside walls

supervisor — a person who manages other workers and plans their work

weld — to join two pieces of metal by heating them until they are soft and stick together

Read More

Graham, Ian. *At a Construction Site.* Machines at Work. Laguna Hills, Calif.: QED Publishing, 2006.

Hyland, Tony. *High-Rise Workers.* Extreme Jobs. North Mankato, Minn.: Smart Apple Media, 2006.

Roth, Susan L. *Hard Hat Area.* New York: Bloomsbury Children's Books, 2004.

Internet Sites

FactHound offers a safe, fun way to find Internet sites related to this book. All of the sites on FactHound have been researched by our staff.

Here's how:

1. Visit *www.facthound.com*

2. Choose your grade level.

3. Type in this book ID **1429612355** for age-appropriate sites. You may also browse subjects by clicking on letters, or by clicking on pictures and words.

4. Click on the **Fetch It** button.

FactHound will fetch the best sites for you!

Index

Word Count: 115
Grade: 1
Early-Intervention Level: 18